No place for a garden

An icy wind teetered trash cans and turned my cheeks to marble. In Vietnam we had no weather like that. Here in Cleveland people call it spring. I walked half a block, then crossed the street and reached the vacant lot.

I stood tall and scouted. I'd never entered the lot before, or wanted to. I did so now, picking my way between tires and trash bags. I nearly stepped on two rats gnawing and froze. Then I told myself that I must show my bravery. I continued farther and chose a spot far from the sidewalk and hidden from view by a rusty refrigerator. I had to keep my project safe.

Acclaim for seedfolks

SEEDFOLKS

by
Paul Fleischman

illustrations by
Judy Pedersen

JOANNA COTLER BOOKS
HarperTrophy®
An Imprint of HarperCollins*Publishers*

Library of Congress Cataloging-in-Publication Data
Fleischman, Paul.
Seedfolks / by Paul Fleischman ; illustrations by Judy Pedersen
p. cm.
"Joanna Cotler books"
Summary: One by one, a number of people of varying ages and
backgrounds transform a trash-filled inner-city lot into a produc-
tive and beautiful garden, and in doing so, the gardeners are them-
selves transformed.
ISBN 0-06-027471-9 — ISBN 0-06-027472-7 (lib. bdg.)
ISBN 0-06-447207-8 (pbk.)
[1. Gardens—Fiction. 2. City and town life—Fiction.
3. Neighborhoods—Fiction.] I. Pedersen, Judy, ill. II. Title.
PZ7.F599233Se 1997   96-26696
[Fic]—dc20   CIP
                                                           AC

Typography by R. Hult
❖
First Harper Trophy edition, 1999
Revised Harper Trophy edition, 2004
Visit us on the World Wide Web!
www.harperchildrens.com

10 11 12 13 OPM 60 59 58 57 56 55 54

For my mother and father

KIM

I stood before our family altar. It was dawn. No one else in the apartment was awake. I stared at my father's photograph—his thin face stern, lips latched tight, his eyes peering permanently to the right. I was nine years old and still hoped that perhaps his eyes might move. Might notice me.

The candles and the incense

sticks, lit the day before to mark his death anniversary, had burned out. The rice and meat offered him were gone. After the evening feast, past midnight, I'd been wakened by my mother's crying. My oldest sister had joined in. My own tears had then come as well, but for a different reason.

I turned from the altar, tiptoed to the kitchen, and quietly drew a spoon from a drawer. I filled my lunch thermos with water and reached into our jar of dried lima beans. Then I walked outside to the street.

The sidewalk was completely empty. It was Sunday, early in April. An icy wind teetered trash cans and turned my cheeks to marble. In Vietnam we had no weather like that. Here in Cleveland people call it spring. I walked half a block, then crossed the street and reached the vacant lot.

I stood tall and scouted. No one was sleeping on the old couch in the middle. I'd never entered the lot before, or wanted to. I did so now, picking my way between tires and trash bags. I nearly stepped on two rats gnawing and froze. Then I told myself that I must show my bravery. I continued farther and chose a spot far from the sidewalk and hidden from view by a rusty refrigerator. I had to keep my project safe.

I took out my spoon and began to dig. The snow had melted, but the ground was hard. After much work, I finished one hole, then a second, then a third. I thought about how my mother and sisters remembered my father, how they knew his face from every angle and held in their fingers the feel of his hands. I had no such memories to cry over. I'd been born eight months after he'd died. Worse, he had no memories of me. When his spirit hovered over our altar, did it even know who I was?

I dug six holes. All his life in Vietnam my father had been a farmer. Here our apartment house had no yard. But in that vacant lot he would see me. He would watch my beans break ground and spread, and would notice with pleasure their pods growing plump. He would see my patience and my hard work. I would show him that I could raise plants, as he had. I would show him that I was his daughter.

My class had sprouted lima beans in paper cups the year before. I now placed a bean in each of the holes. I covered them up, pressing the soil down firmly with my fingertips. I opened my thermos and watered them all. And I vowed to myself that those beans would thrive.

ANA

I do love to sit and look out the window. Why do I need TV when I have forty-eight apartment windows to watch across the vacant lot, and a sliver of Lake Erie? I've seen history out this window. So much. I was four when we moved here in 1919. The fruit-sellers' carts and coal wagons were pulled down the street by horses back then. I used to stand just here and watch the coal brought up by the handsome lad from Groza, the village my parents were born in. Gibb Street was mainly Rumanians back then. It was *"Adio"*—"Good-bye"—in all the shops when you left. Then the Rumanians started leaving. They weren't the first, or the last. This has always been a working-class neighborhood. It's like a cheap hotel—you stay until you've got enough money to leave. A lot of Slovaks and Italians moved in next. Then Negro families in the Depression. Gibb Street became the line between the blacks and the whites, like a border between countries. I watched it happen, through this very window.

I lived over in Cleveland Heights for eighteen years, then I moved back in to take care of my parents. That border moved too. Most all the whites left. Then the steel mills and factories closed and *everybody* left, like rats. Buildings abandoned. Men with no work drinking from nine to five instead, down there in the lot. Always the sirens, people killing each other. Now I see families from Mexico and Cambodia and countries I don't know, twelve people sometimes in one apartment. New languages in the shops and on the street. These new people leave when they can, like the others. I'm the only one staying. It's so. Staying and staring out this same window.

This spring I looked out and I saw something strange. Down in the lot, a little black-haired girl, hiding behind that refrigerator. She was working at the dirt and looking around suspiciously all the time. Then I realized. She was burying something.

I never had children of my own, but I've seen enough in that lot to know she was mixed up in something she shouldn't be. And after twenty years typing for the Parole department, I just about knew what she'd buried. Drugs most likely, or money, or a gun. The next moment, she disappeared like a rabbit.

I thought of calling up the police. Then I saw her there the next morning, and I decided I'd solve this case myself. We had a long spell of rain then. I didn't set eyes on her once. Then the weather turned warm and I saw her twice more, always in the morning, on her way to school. She was crouched down with her back to me so I couldn't see just what she was doing. My curiosity was like a fever inside me. Then one morning she was there, glancing about, and she looked straight up at this window.

I pulled my head back behind the curtain. I wasn't sure if she'd seen me. If she had, she wouldn't leave her treasure buried long. Then I knew I'd have to dig it up before she did.

I waited an hour after she left. Then I took an old butter knife and my cane and hobbled down all three flights of stairs. I worked my way through that awful jungle of junk and finally came to her spot. I stooped down. It was wet there and easy digging. I hacked and dug, but didn't find anything, except for a large white bean. I tried a new spot and found another, then a third. Then the truth of it slapped me full in the face. I said to myself, "What have you *done*?" Two beans had roots. I knew I'd done them harm. I felt like I'd read through her secret diary and had ripped out a page without meaning to. I laid those beans right back in the ground, as gently as sleeping babies. Then I patted the soil as smooth as could be.

The next morning she was back. I peeked around the curtain. She didn't look up here or give any sign that she noticed something wrong. I could see her clearly this time. She reached a hand into her schoolbag. Then she pulled out a jar, unscrewed the lid, and poured out water onto the ground.

That afternoon I bought some binoculars.

WENDELL

My phone doesn't ring much, which suits me fine. That's how I got the news about our boy, shot dead like a dog in the street. And the word, last year, about my wife's car wreck. I can't hear a phone and not jerk inside. When Ana called I was still asleep. Phone calls that wake me up are the worst.

"Get up here quick!" she says. I live on the ground floor and watch out for her a little. We're the only white people left in the building. I ran up the stairs. I could tell it was serious. I prayed I wouldn't find her dead. When I got there, she looked perfectly fine. She dragged me over to the window. "Look down there!" she says. "They're dying!"

"What?" I yelled back.

"The plants!" she says.

I was mad. She gave me some binoculars and told me all about the Chinese girl. I found the plants and got them in focus. There were four of them in a row, still little. They were wilted. Leaves flopped flat on the ground.

"What are they?" she asked.

"Some kind of beans." I grew up on a little farm in Kentucky. "But she planted 'em way too early. She's lucky those seeds even came up."

"But they did," said Ana. "And it's up to us to save them."

It was a weekend in May and hot. You'd have thought that those beans were hers. They needed water, especially in that heat. She said the girl hadn't come in four days—sick, probably, or gone out of town. Ana had twisted her ankle and couldn't manage the stairs. She pointed to a pitcher. "Fill that up and soak them good. Quick now."

School janitors take too much bossing all week to listen to an extra helping on weekends. I stared at her one long moment, then took my time about filling the pitcher.

I walked down the stairs and into the lot and found the girl's plants. You don't plant beans till the weather's hot. Then I saw what had kept her seeds from freezing. The refrigerator in front of them had bounced the sunlight back on the soil, heating it up like an oven. I bent down and gave the dirt a feel. It was hard packed and light colored. I studied the plants. Leaves shaped like spades in a deck of cards. Definitely beans. I scraped up a ring of dirt around the first plant, to hold the water and any rain that fell. I picked up the pitcher and poured the water slowly. Then I heard something move and spun around. The girl was there, stone-still, ten feet away, holding her own water jar.

She hadn't seen me behind the refrigerator. She looked afraid for her life. Maybe she thought I'd jump up and grab her. I gave her a smile and showed her that I was just giving her plants some water. This made her eyes go even bigger. I stood up slowly and backed away. I smiled again. She watched me leave. We never spoke one word.

I walked back there that evening and checked on the beans. They'd picked themselves up and were looking fine. I saw that she'd made a circle of dirt around the other three plants. Out of nowhere the words from the Bible came into my head: "And a little child shall lead them." I didn't know why at first. Then I did. There's plenty about my life I can't change. Can't bring the dead back to life on this earth. Can't make the world loving and kind. Can't change myself into a millionaire. But a patch of ground in this trashy lot—I *can* change that. Can change it big. Better to put my time into that than moaning about the other all day. That little grammar-school girl showed me that.

The lot had buildings on three sides. I walked around and picked myself out a spot that wouldn't be shaded too much. I dragged the garbage off to the side and tossed out the biggest pieces of broken glass. I looked over my plot, squatted down, and fingered the soil awhile.

That Monday I brought a shovel home from work.

GONZALO

The older you are, the younger you get when you move to the United States.

They don't teach you that equation in school. Big Brain, Mr. Smoltz, my eighth-grade math teacher, hasn't even heard of it. It's not in *Gateway to Algebra*. It's Garcia's Equation. I'm the Garcia.

Two years after my father

and I moved here from Guatemala I could speak English. I learned it on the playground and watching lots of TV. Don't believe what people say—cartoons make you *smart*. But my father, he worked all day in a kitchen with Mexicans and Salvadorans. His English was worse than a kindergartner's. He would only buy food at the *bodega* down the block. Outside of there he lowered his eyes and tried to get by on mumbles and smiles. He didn't want strangers to hear his mistakes. So he used me to make phone calls and to talk to the landlady and to buy things in stores where you had to use English. He got younger. I got older.

Then my younger brothers and mother and Tío Juan, her uncle, came north and joined us. Tío Juan was the oldest man in his pueblo. But here he became a little baby.

He'd been a farmer, but here he couldn't work. He couldn't sit out in the plaza and talk—there *aren't* any plazas here, and if you sit out in public some gang driving by might use you for target practice. He couldn't understand TV. So he wandered around the apartment all day, in and out of rooms, talking to himself, just like a kid in diapers.

One morning he wandered outside and down the street. My mother practically fainted. He doesn't speak Spanish, just an Indian language. I finally found him standing in front of the beauty parlor, staring through the glass at a woman with a drier over her head. He must have wondered what weird planet he'd moved to. I led him home, holding his hand, the way you would with a three-year-old. Since then I'm supposed to baby-sit him after school.

One afternoon I was watching TV,

getting smart on *The Brady Bunch.* Suddenly I looked up. He was gone. I checked the halls on all five floors of the apartment house. I ran to the street. He wasn't in the *bodega* or the pawnshop. I called his name, imagining my mother's face when she found out he'd fallen through a manhole or been run over. I turned the corner, looking for the white straw hat he always wore. Two blocks down I spotted it. I flew down the sidewalk and found him standing in front of a vacant lot, making gestures to a man with a shovel.

I took his hand, but he pulled me through the trash and into the lot. I recognized the man with the shovel—he was the janitor at my old school. He had a little garden planted. Different shades of green leaves were coming up in rows. Tío Juan was smiling and trying to tell him something. The man couldn't understand him and finally went back to digging. I turned Tío Juan around and led him home.

That night he told my mother all about it. She was the only one who could understand him. When she got home from work the next day she asked me to take him back there. I did. He studied the sun. Then the soil. He felt it, then smelled it, then actually tasted it. He chose a spot not too far from the sidewalk. Where my mother changed busses she'd gone into a store and bought him a trowel and four packets of seeds. I cleared the trash, he turned the soil. I wished we were farther from the street and I was praying that none of my friends or girlfriends or enemies saw me. Tío Juan didn't even notice people—he was totally wrapped up in the work.

He showed me exactly how far apart

the rows should be and how deep. He couldn't read the words on the seed packets, but he knew from the pictures what seeds were inside. He poured them into his hand and smiled. He seemed to recognize them, like old friends. Watching him carefully sprinkling them into the troughs he'd made, I realized that I didn't know anything about growing food and that he knew everything. I stared at his busy fingers, then his eyes. They were focused, not faraway or confused. He'd changed from a baby back into a man.

LEONA

Mama believed in doctors, but not Granny. Not even if they were black. *No, ma'am.* I grew up in her house, back in Atlanta. She drank down a big cup of goldenrod tea every morning, with a nutmeg floating in it, and declared she didn't need no other medicine. Dr. Bates tried to sell her his iron pills and told her straight out that that tea of hers would raise her blood pressure and burst her heart. He passed away that very same summer. Next doctor said it would give her brain fever. He died on his fiftieth birthday, I believe, right during the party. Had him a real nice funeral, later. Granny lived to ninety-nine, by her count. She kept a scrapbook with the obituaries of all the doctors she outlived and could recite the list of names by heart, like a chapter out of Genesis. We took to going to their funerals right regular over the years. She always laid some goldenrod on their graves.

I was thinking about her one day, walking home from the grocery store on Gibb Street. Then I came to the vacant lot and saw three people in different parts of it. I thought maybe they were looking for money. Turned out they had shovels, not metal detectors. When I saw they had little gardens going, I said to myself, "I believe I'll plant me a patch of goldenrod right here."

There was a man standing and watching from the sidewalk and a girl looking down out a window. There were probably lots of folks who'd want to grow something, just like me. Then I studied all the trash on the ground. Don't know why anyone called that lot "vacant." The garbage was piled high as your waist, some of it from the neighborhood and some dropped off by outside people. The ones who don't want to pay at the dump, or got dangerous chemicals, or think we're such slobs down here we won't mind another load of junk. We can't get City Hall to *pick up* our trash, but we got it *delivered* just fine. The smell's enough to curl up a crocodile's nose, especially in the summer. The gardeners had made some trails through it. But I knew precious few would join 'em until that mess was hauled away. Looking at it, I knew this wasn't a job for no wheelbarrow. This was a job for the telephone.

I marched on home. I've got two kids in a high school that has more guns than books, so I know all about complaining to officials and such about things that need changing. Next morning was Monday. At nine o'clock I drank me a tall glass of water. I knew I'd be having to say the same thing to fifteen or twenty government folks. I put Miles on the CD player and stretched out on the bed. Might as well be comfortable when you're on hold. Then I opened the phone book and started in dialing.

You ever watch a sax player close? They push down a key and way at the other end of the instrument something moves. That's what I was looking for—the key that would make that trash disappear. I tried the City of

Cleveland, then Cuyahoga County, then the State of Ohio, and finally the U.S. government. Six and a half hours later I found out the lot was owned by the city. But the people running Cleveland don't usually come down here, unless they take a wrong turn on the freeway. You can't measure the distance between my block and City Hall in miles.

Just the same, I kept working on it the next day. That Citizens' Information Center told me to call the Public Health Department. They sent me to someone else. They're all trained to be slippery as snakes. And to be out to lunch, to not return messages, and to keep folks on hold till they get gray and die. I had the feeling I was getting farther from the key I needed instead of closer. Then on the third day, I thought on it. When people talk to you on the phone, you're nothing but a voice. And when you're on hold you're not even that. I had to make myself real to 'em.

That morning I took a bus downtown and walked into the Public Health Department. Told about the trash all over again to this dolled-up receptionist. Let her see me up close and personal and hear me loud and clear. She just told me to sit down with the others waiting. I did. Then I opened the garbage bag I'd picked up in the lot on my way.

The smell that came out of it made you think of hog pens and maggots and kitchen scraps from back when Nixon was president. It was amazing how quick people noticed it, including that receptionist. And even more amazing how quick I was called in to have a meeting with someone. I was *definitely* real to them now. I brought that bag along with me into the meeting, to keep it that way.

SAM

I saw people on the sidewalk, watching something. I crossed to join them, like a cat who smells herring. Men in jumpsuits, from the jail I think, were clearing the lot. Unbelievable. The woman beside me told me the land was for anyone who wanted a gar-den. Even more unbeliev-able. The word "paradise"

came out of my mouth, without thinking. The woman looked at me strange. It's a hobby with me, studying words. I looked at the three walls surrounding the lot, then at a garden coming up beautiful, planted there close to the sidewalk. "Paradise" comes from a Persian word. It means "walled park." I told the woman that. This time she gave me a little smile. I smiled back. That's my occupation.

You've seen fishermen mending the rips in their nets. That's what I do, only with people. I used to try to patch up the whole world. For thirty-six years I worked for different groups, promoting world government, setting up conferences on pacifism, raising money, stuffing envelopes. Not that I've given up the fight. I've just switched battlefields, from the entire planet to this corner of Cleveland. Sometimes I think I've actually had more effect on the world since I retired. What do I do? I smile at people, especially black people and the ones from different countries. I get 'em looking up at me instead of down or off to the side. I start up conversations in lines and on the bus and with cashiers. People see I'm friendly, no matter what they've heard about whites or Jews. If I'm lucky, I get 'em talking to each other. Sewing up the rips in the neighborhood.

I hadn't had a garden since I was a kid. I wanted one now, only this time I was seventy-eight to be exact, and in no condition to dig up the soil. So I hired a teenager, Puerto Rican, who said he knew where he could get a shovel. He knew he'd have to do a good job to be paid. He worked that soil until it flowed through your fingers like silk. I paid him well and offered him a row. He wanted to grow marijuana, to sell. A real businessman. We discussed this. We finally compromised on pumpkins, after I explained how much he could probably get for them at Halloween, not to mention the advantages of staying out of jail. He was new to the neighborhood. We chatted back and forth. Squatting there in the cool of the evening, planting our seeds, a few other people working, a robin singing out strong all the while, it seemed to me that we were in truth in Paradise, a small Garden of Eden.

In the Bible, though, there's a river in Eden. Here, we had none. Not even a spigot anywhere close by. Nothing. People had to lug their own water, in buckets or milk jugs or soda containers. Water is heavy as bricks, trust me. And new seeds have to be always moist. And in all of June it didn't rain but four days. The result? People bent over like coolies, walking sometimes three or four blocks, a gallon jug in each hand, complaining all the time about the water. Mine I had hauled by a third-grader with a wagon. The contest I started came later.

Water aside, we had other problems. People in the garden told friends and relatives. The lot was big, there was plenty of room. But when newcomers joined, at least at the beginning, they could usually get a spot near people they knew. One Saturday, when the garden was fullest, I stood up a minute to straighten my back. And what did I see? With a few exceptions, the blacks on one side, the whites on another, the Central Americans and Asians toward the back. The garden was a copy of the neighborhood. I guess I shouldn't have been surprised. A duck gives birth to a duckling, not a moose. Each group kept to itself, spoke its own language, and grew its own special crops. One man even put up a pole and flew the Philippine flag above his plot.

Then there was the garbage. A few well brought-up people in the buildings around the lot still used it for a trash can. Just couldn't get out of the habit. They emptied their ashtrays out the windows and tossed out all sorts of stuff. One day a bottle came down, like a meteor. A man picked it up and threw it back, straight through the window it came out of. A minute later, five more flew out. Next, I thought to myself, come gunshots. Instead, thank God, it was only shouting.

That crazy homeless man, the one who used to sleep on the broken-down couch— he also missed the lot being a dump. He showed up, saw his couch had been taken, and started ripping out people's plants. The police had to come. Some people started worrying, looking ahead to ripe beans and tomatoes and thinking about strangers coming in. That week, a man put chicken wire around his garden, five feet high, complete with a little gate and padlock. The week after that someone built a board fence. Then came the first KEEP OUT sign. Then, the crowning achievement—barbed wire.

God, who made Eden, also wrecked the Tower of Babel, by dividing people. From Paradise, the garden was turning back into Cleveland.

VIRGIL

My father, he always has a smile on his face and a plan moving in his head. We were standing together on the sidewalk while the men were clearing the lot. I was watching the rats running for their lives. They were shooting off every which way. A couple of dealers came over, the ones always bragging about how bad they are. A rat ran right up one of their legs. The dude screamed, just like women do with a mouse in cartoons, only louder. Shook his leg like his toe was being electrocuted. That rat flew off and dove down a storm drain. I looked at my father. That's when I saw that he hadn't paid the rat any mind. Hadn't even turned his head. His eyes were stuck completely on the garden land being uncovered. He had a two-foot-wide smile on his face.

My father drove a bus back in Haiti. Here he drives a taxi. That night he drove himself way across town to borrow two shovels from a friend of his. The next morning was the first day without school. I was done with fifth grade forever. I'd planned on sleeping till noon to celebrate. But when it was still half dark my father shook my shoulder. School was over, but that garden was just starting.

We walked down and picked out a place to dig up. The ground was packed so hard, the tip of my shovel bounced off it like a pogo stick. We tried three spots till we found one we liked. Then we walked back and forth, picking out broken glass, like chickens pecking seeds. After that we turned the soil. We were always digging up more trash—bolts and screws and pieces of brick. That's how I found the locket. It was shaped like a heart and covered with rust, with a broken chain. I got it open. Inside was this tiny photo of a girl. She was white, with a sad-looking face. She had on this hat with flowers on it. I don't know why I kept it instead of tossing it on our trash pile.

It seemed like hours and hours before we had the ground finished. We rested a while. Then my father asked if I was ready.

I thought he meant ready to plant our seeds. But instead, we turned another square of ground. Then another after that. Then three more after that. My father hadn't been smiling to himself about some little garden. He was thinking of a farm, to make money. I'd seen a package of seeds for pole beans and hoped that's what we'd grow. They get so tall that the man in the picture was picking 'em way at the top of a ladder. But my father said no. He was always asking people in his cab about how to get rich. One of 'em told him that fancy restaurants paid lots of money for this baby lettuce, smaller than the regular kind, to use in rich folks' salads. The fresher it was, the higher the price. My father planned to pick it and then race it right over in his cab. Running red lights if he had to.

Lettuce seeds are smaller than sand. I

felt embarrassed, planting so much ground. No one else's garden was a quarter the size of ours. Suddenly I saw Miss Fleck. I hardly recognized her in jeans. She was the strictest teacher in Ohio. I'd had her for third grade. She pronounced every letter in every word, and expected you to talk the same way. She was tall and even blacker than my father. No slouching in your seat in her class or any kind of rudeness. The other teachers seemed afraid of her too. She walked over just when we finished planting.

"Well, Virgil," she said. "You seem to have claimed quite a large *plantation* here."

That's just what I was afraid of hearing. I looked away from her, down at our sticks. We'd put 'em in the ground and run string around 'em, cutting our land up into six pieces. I didn't know why, till my father stepped forward.

"Actually, madam, only this very first area here is ours," he said. He had on his biggest smile. He must have remembered her. "The others we have planted at the request of relatives who have no tools or who live too far."

"Really, now," said Miss Fleck.

"Yes, madam," said my father. He pointed at the closest squares of land. "My brother Antoine. My auntie, Anne-Marie."

My eyes opened wide. They both lived in Haiti. I stared at my father, but he just kept smiling. His finger pointed farther to the left. "My Uncle Philippe." He lived in New York. "My wife's father." He died last year. "And her sister." My mother didn't have any sisters. I looked at my father's smiling face. I'd never watched an adult lie before.

"And what did your *extended* family of

gardeners ask you to plant?" said Miss Fleck.

"Lettuce," said my father. "All lettuce."

"What a coincidence," she said back. She just stood, then walked over to her own garden. I'm pretty sure she didn't believe him. But what principal could she send him to?

That lettuce was like having a new baby in the family. And I was like its mother. I watered it in the morning if my father was still out driving. It was supposed to come up in seven days, but it didn't. My father couldn't figure out why. Neither of us knew anything about plants. This wrinkled old man in a straw hat tried to show me something when I poured out the water. He spoke some language, but it sure wasn't English. I didn't get what he was babbling about, till the lettuce finally came up in wavy lines and bunches instead of straight rows. I'd washed the seeds out of their places.

The minute it came up, it started to wilt. It was like a baby always crying for its milk. I got sick of hauling bottles of water in our shopping cart, like I was some old lady. Then the heat came. The leaves shriveled up. Some turned yellow. That lettuce was dying.

My father practically cried, looking at it. He'd stop by in his cab when he could, with two five-gallon water containers riding in the back instead of passengers. Then bugs started eating big holes in the plants. I couldn't see anyone buying them from us. My father had promised we'd make enough money to buy me an eighteen-speed bike. I was counting on it. I'd already told my friends. My father asked all his passengers what to do. His cab was like a library for him. Finally, one of 'em told him that spring or fall was the time to grow lettuce, that the summer was too hot for it. My father wasn't smiling when he told us.

I couldn't believe it. I stomped outside. I could feel that eighteen-speed slipping away. I was used to seeing kids lying and making mistakes, but not grown-ups. I was mad at my father. Then I sort of felt sorry for him.

That night I pulled out the locket. I opened it up and looked at the picture. We'd studied Greek myths in school that year. In our book, the goddess of crops and the earth had a sad mouth and flowers around her, just like the girl in the locket. I scraped off the rust with our dish scrubber and shined up that locket as bright as I could get it. Then I opened it up, just a crack. Then I whispered, "Save our lettuce," to the girl.

SAE YOUNG

Always many people in my house when I was young. Five sisters. Many friends. I always like being with people. Then I leave Korea with my husband to come to America, for work. We buy dry cleaning shop, live next block. Dry cleaning shop better than restaurant. Don't have to speak English too much and only work six days. We work together, seven until seven. At night I sew alterations. We save all for children's college, so they can have easier life. But no children come. Very many years we hope, but still alone. Then my husband die. Heart attack. Thirty-seven years old. Now all alone, except for friends. I hire woman to work in shop. One afternoon when she gone, a man walk into shop with coat to clean. Under coat he has gun. He take out money, then push me down. He yelling at me. Very bad words. Then he kick me. Break cheekbone. Then he kick me again, head hit hard against wall and I go to sleep.

When I wake up, I no more like to be with people, like before. Afraid of everyone, all the time. I don't leave apartment for two months. Neighbor buys food for me at store. I don't open door if someone knocks, even friends—only for food. Afraid to walk on sidewalk with people. I hire Korean man to run dry cleaning shop. I never go in. That happen two years ago. Very slowly, I get better. I go to store and buy my food, but very fast. Then not so fast. Very lonely, but still afraid. Then I pass by garden.

Vietnamese girl was working there, picking beautiful lima beans. A man and a woman on other side, talking over row of corn. Hear man say his wife give him hoe for birthday. I want to be with people again. Next day I go back and dig small garden. Nobody talk to me that day. But just be near people, nice people, feel good, like next to fire in winter.

Very hot and humid in July. Most people come early in evening, after work, when air is cool. People watering and pulling weeds.

Even if don't talk to anyone, sound of people working almost like conversation, all around. People visit friends. I listen to voices. Feel very safe. Then man walk over and ask about peppers. I grow hot peppers, like in Korea. First time that someone talk to me. I was so glad, have trouble talking.

That man named Sam. He's American man and talk to everyone. Very smart. When people all the time complain about carrying water, he start contest. He said how adults couldn't solve problem, let children try. He say he give twenty dollars to child under twelve who has best idea. He write this on paper and nail paper to post close to sidewalk.

One week to contest. Kids out of school, walk around, see paper, tell friends. On Saturday, everyone bring plans. Sam has wooden box, let each one stand on it and tell idea. One girl live in apartment by garden. She say she'll open window, people give her containers, she'll fill them with water. Then mother interrupt, say water bill too much. Boy say use water from fire hydrant. Another say run hose from Lake Erie. Many ideas. Sam explain how much money each one cost. Then little black girl say to let rain from spouts go into garbage cans. Everyone look. Three different spouts on walls of building around garden. Just have to take off bottom part of spout. Sam give girl twenty dollars. Everyone clap. Other people give money to buy garbage cans.

Next day, thunderstorm. Cans almost full. Little girl there, very proud. Someone bring three old pots to scoop water out of cans. Hard to pour into narrow containers. I quick go to store. Buy three funnels to make much easier filling containers. I put one by each garbage can. That day I see man use my funnel. Then woman. Then many people. Feel very glad inside. Feel part of garden. Almost like family.

CURTIS

Deltoids—awesome. Pecs—check 'em out. Quads—now playing on a body near you. Can't help being born with this body, or living three doors down from Kapp's Gym. Can't stop people calling me Atlas or Ceps. That's short for Biceps R Us. Actually, I started that name. But that was before Lateesha cut me loose.

We had us a real nice thing going. She was a few years older than me, always talking about having a family, living in a house in the country, like her aunt's place in Michigan. I wasn't really listening too hard. I was twenty-three. With this body, I had other girls hanging on me at the time. Some of 'em I just couldn't brush off. When Lateesha found out, she slammed the door in my face so hard the paint cracked.

You don't know what you got till it's gone. All that was five years ago. I've caught up with her now. Done fooling around. She was looking for a husband, and now I'm looking for a wife. I moved back from Cincinnati in May and ran into her brother the first day. Said she's still single. Same third-floor apartment. But when I came up to her on the street, she turned her back. Wouldn't let me explain. Twice it happened. No chance for words. So I decided to give her some deeds instead.

She lives straight across the street from the garden. I staked out a spot right by the sidewalk, where she could look down and see it. Then I came home with six little tomato plants in plastic containers. She had a serious thing for tomatoes. She'd put a monster slice on a piece of bread and call it a sandwich. She'd even bite into 'em, just like apples. Always talking about eating 'em out of her aunt's garden when she was a kid and how she wanted to grow 'em someday. She probably thought I forgot all that. I planted 'em right there in front of her eyes, to show her I hadn't, that I was waiting for her.

I got the biggest—beefsteak tomatoes. I could see 'em in my mind, bright as traffic lights, flashing at her across the street. I'd never grown anything before. I got into it. Every day something new. The first flower bud. Then those first yellow flowers. Then the tomatoes growing right behind 'em. This old man with no teeth and a straw hat showed me how to tie the plants up to stakes. Then someone else told me all their diseases. That got me worrying. What if all my plants started wilting? Or caught blight and died? That wasn't any message I'd want her to see.

I started coming straight from work to check 'em. I noticed every hole in every leaf. I picked off bugs, pulled out weeds, and I gave 'em lots of that fertilizer called Tomato Food, like somebody told me. From little green marbles, those tomatoes started growing. Then they started getting orange. Then they went to red. I kept looking up at Lateesha's window, wanting her to see it too. The only faces looking back were the drunks that hang out under her place. That liquor store's all boarded up, but they still suck on their bottles there anyway. They liked to call me "field slave" and "share-cropper." Ask how Massa's crops is doing. I could have banged their heads together and shut 'em up, but I didn't. That was part of the point of the tomatoes. I was showing Lateesha that just cause I got muscles don't mean I'm some jungle beast. I stopped working out and stopped going out with no shirt, no matter how hot it was. When some chicks would be walking by and see me there and say "Looking fine," I knew they meant me but I'd point to my biggest tomato and say back "Sure is." My homies all laughed to see me out there. Stopped calling me Ceps. Started in calling me Tomato. I just smiled.

Those tomatoes got big as billiard balls. One day when I checked 'em, my biggest one, the one I'd been watching closest, was gone. The next day, another one gone. It wasn't insects that took 'em. I was mad. They weren't even all the way ripe yet. My plants were right there by the sidewalk. I put chicken wire around 'em, and even on top, but people could still reach in if they tried. I couldn't guard 'em day and night. Then Royce showed up, just in time.

You drop bread on the ground and birds come out of nowhere. Same with that garden. People just appeared, people you didn't know were there. Royce was like that. Except that he didn't *want* nobody knowing he was there. One of the gardeners saw that her pile of grass clippings was all spread out. Had a sort of human print in it. He'd been sleeping there nights and leaving early. One morning he slept late. I'm the one who found him. He was fifteen, black, built big—looked like I did. His face was banged up. Said his father did it and threw him out. He didn't want to go back. I bought him breakfast and we made us a deal.

I found him a place closer to my tomatoes but hidden by somebody's corn, so the cops wouldn't see him sacked out. I bought him a brand new sleeping bag. I gave him money for food that week. Then I picked up a pitchfork for three dollars at a junk shop. His part of the deal was that if he saw or heard *anyone* mess with my tomatoes, he'd come at 'em full speed, holding the pitchfork.

That was my best shot protecting 'em at night. For daytime, when Royce was gone, I painted a sign that said "Lateesha's

Tomatoes." It was big. I put it right there in front of the plants, facing the sidewalk. If people know something belongs to a person instead of the city or the U.S. government they're more likely to leave it be.

When I'd pounded it in, I filled up my water can. Walking back, I looked up at her window. As still as a cat, behind that lace curtain, there was her face, staring down at the sign.

NORA

I always try to get Mr. Myles out for a walk and a taste of fresh air. I don't know about his other nurses. I expect that it's because I'm British. Back in England you'd see mothers pushing infants in prams through winter gales. I expect as well it was the sight of my own father, vegetating in his chair by the fire. We mustn't stop living before our time. So I'm forever telling Mr. Myles.

It was a midsummer morning and I was pushing his wheelchair up Gibb Street, a new route for us. The view, I'll admit, is less than uplifting. Half the storefronts seem to be empty. Mr. Myles must remember a very different scene. His landlady says he's lived here many years. As he lost his speech with his second stroke, he can't tell me himself. He's a mystery. Lately his interest in the world had declined. I'd stop before a store window to let him see himself—he has the dignified head of an African chief—only to find that he'd fallen asleep. I realized that his time might be near. And then, that morning, rolling along the sidewalk, suddenly his arm came up.

He wanted to stop. I obliged him at once. To our left was a lot in which a few bold pioneers had planted gardens. We remained several minutes, watching two Asian women hoeing, then continued on. Immediately, back up went his arm. I came around and looked at him. He twisted and pointed toward the garden. I turned the wheelchair and headed back. I could see his nostrils taking in the smell of the soil. We reached the lot. His arm commanded me to enter. Over the narrow, bumpy path we went, his nose and eyes working. Some remembered scent was pulling him. He was a salmon traveling upstream through his past.

That first day we simply watched the others. We might have been strolling through a miniature city. Some plots sported brick pathways and flower borders, while others looked haphazard. One had a gate that was in fact a car door. Within, beans climbed a propped-up set of bedsprings.

A hummingbird feeder, a barbecue grill, a gardening hat hanging from a nail—there were many such domestic touches. I was entranced. I determined that Mr. Myles should do more than simply watch, wheelchair or no.

I worked on the problem in my head. Two days later, driving to his apartment, I stopped at the garden and unloaded a large plastic trash barrel and a shovel. I wheeled him up an hour later, used my pocketknife to cut holes in the bottom of the barrel for drainage, and built up a fine sweat shoveling in dirt. I'd brought with me a dozen seed packets. Mr. Myles chose the flowers decisively, ignoring the vegetables. Was he recalling his mother's flower garden? His history was unknowable. I pushed him as close to the barrel as I could. Thirty minutes later he'd planted hollyhocks, poppies, and snapdragons. Riding home afterward, he smelled the dirt on his fingers with satisfaction.

That small circle of earth became a second home to both of us. Gardening boring? Never! It has suspense, tragedy, startling developments—a soap opera growing out of the ground. I'd forgotten that tremolo of expectation produced by a tiny forest of sprouts. What a marvelous sight it was to behold Mr. Myles' furrowed black face inspecting his smooth-skinned young, just arrived in the world he'd shortly leave. His eyes gained back some of their life. He weeded and watered with great concentration. A fact bobbed up from my memory, that the ancient Egyptians prescribed walking through a garden as a cure for the mad. It was a mind-altering drug we took daily.

We were rather alone there, off to one

side. Our most common visitors were the cats. They were attracted by the aroma of fish, the work of a child who'd copied the Pilgrims of old and buried sardines with her seeds. Then our solitary status ended, as a result of a downpour. When the rain came that day, the other gardeners all ran in the same direction, as if in a fire drill. We followed and found them sheltered beneath a shoe store's overhang two doors down, apparently their customary refuge. The small dry space forced us together. In fifteen minutes we'd met them all and soon knew the whole band of regulars.

Most were old. Many grew plants from their native lands—huge Chinese melons, ginger, cilantro, a green the Jamaicans call calaloo, and many more. Pantomime was often required to get over language barriers. Yet we were all subject to the same weather and pests, the same neighborhood, and the same parental emotions toward our plants. If we happened to miss two or three days, people stopped by on our return to ask about Mr. Myles' health. We, like our seeds, were now planted in the garden.

I told all this to out-of-town guests, then took them up Terminal Tower. We got off at the observation deck on the forty-second floor to find that the garden, which loomed so large to its tenders, was hopelessly hidden from view by buildings. I looked at all the tourists, who'd no notion it existed, who thought they were seeing all of Cleveland, and restrained myself from pointing and shouting out, "The Gibb Street garden is there!"

MARICELA

If you're Mexican, the Cubans and Puerto Ricans hate you because they think you snuck in illegally and they didn't. Which they would have if they could have walked. If you're a teenager, the whole world hates you. If you're a pregnant teenager, people think you should be burned at the stake. I'm a Mexican, pregnant sixteen-year-old. So shoot me and get it over with.

I wouldn't actually care if you did. In a way I'm already dead. I used to be really, really hot. Because of the baby I'm as fat as a wrestler. I dropped out, I've been to exactly zero parties, and I've been asked out exactly zero times, including by the scum who got me pregnant. My parents were mad. They wanted me to graduate. But abortion or adoption—forget it. Then they got sort of excited about it. They both love little babies. Not me. They started praying for it every night, while I was begging my body to miscarry.

Three of us from my high school got into this program for pregnant teens. They give you rides to the doctor and help with getting your G.E.D. at home. Great. Except that Penny, the woman we see, saw the community garden and got the program its own spot, to give us practice taking care of something and to let us witness "the miracle of life." And to try to keep us from eating our babies alive or dropping them into dumpsters.

It was already the middle of summer, so she had us plant radishes since they grow fast. All three of us hate radishes. As soon as the little green leaves came up a gopher or something wiped 'em out. So much for the miracle of life. I didn't tell Penny I was hoping the same thing happened to my baby. She's so cheerful I never could. *She's* not puking or getting as big as a blimp—*no wonder* she's always smiling.

After the radishes came squash, then Swiss chard, which nobody knew how to eat. I was in my seventh month. I hated the bending. We all complained, but Penny just smiled. The rest of us called working there the Chain Gang. I hated the feel of dirt under my nails. One afternoon Yolanda broke two of her fancy, painted, expensive nails and cursed out loud for ten minutes. Penny couldn't shut her up. Then another woman came over and gave us this long lecture about the word "decorum." I couldn't believe my eyes—it was my old third-grade teacher, Miss Fleck. I prayed she wouldn't recognize me, but naturally she did, and asked me all the usual questions. I should have had the answers printed up on a card to hand out. The next week, when some man threw a can out his window, which landed about a foot from my head, Miss Fleck figured out what apartment he was in, walked up, and yelled at him like he was a kid. She treated the whole world like her classroom.

Different people came to our part of the

garden for different reasons. This Puerto Rican kid had these pumpkin plants that kept getting into ours. Which gave him an excuse to walk right past me and talk to Dolores, who was fifteen and pretty and still didn't look pregnant. I couldn't wait for her to get huge. Sometimes this black guy ran through our garden. He couldn't take time to go around. He grew lettuce, or tried to. Most of it was dead. He'd drive up in a cab, slam on the brakes like the Pope just stepped in front of him, run through our squash, cut a bunch of lettuce, and run back with it in a bucket of water. Then he'd peel out, leaving lots of rubber. Then there were the people who came by to give us different things. Vegetables that they'd grown and thought we should eat, which we always gave away later. Advice on growing our stupid Swiss chard. Advice on giving birth and raising kids, which I tuned out as soon as they started.

One day in August it was just me and Penny. This black woman, Leona, who had a garden and talked to us, came over and gave me some flowers she'd grown. They were yellow. She called 'em goldenrod and she said if I made 'em into tea it would help me with the delivery. She knew I didn't want to be pregnant. I could talk to her about it. That day it was almost too humid to talk. The windows around the garden were open and you could hear ten different TV's and radios. A storm was coming. The thunder was getting closer. And then it hit—*bam!* Then all the TV's and radios went off. So did the lights. It was a power failure.

It was quiet in the garden without all the noise. So quiet it was weird. I looked around.

An old man near us was slowly picking cucumbers, like nothing had happened. "Whole city shuts down, but the garden just keeps going," Leona said. She talked on, how plants don't run on electricity or clock time, how none of nature did. How nature ran on sunlight and rain and the seasons, and how I was part of that system. The words sort of put me into a daze. My body was part of nature. I was related to bears, to dinosaurs, to plants, to things that were a million years old. It hit me that this system was much older and stronger than the other. She said how it wasn't some disgrace to be part of it. She said it was an honor. I stared at the squash plants. It was a world in there. It seemed like I could actually see the leaves and flowers growing and changing. I was in that weird daze. And for just that minute I stopped wishing my baby would die.

AMIR

In India we have many vast cities, just as in America. There, too, you are one among millions. But there at least you know your neighbors. Here, one cannot say that. The object in America is to avoid contact, to treat all as foes unless they're known to be friends. Here you have a million crabs living in a million crevices.

When I saw the garden for the first time, so green among the dark brick buildings, I thought back to my parents' Persian rug. It showed climbing vines, rivers and waterfalls, grapes, flower beds, singing birds, everything a desert dweller might dream of. Those rugs were indeed portable gardens. In the summers in Delhi, so very hot, my sisters and I would lie upon it and try to press ourselves into its world. The garden's green was as soothing to the eye as the deep blue of that rug. I'm aware of color—I manage a fabric store. But the garden's greatest benefit, I feel, was not relief to the eyes, but to make the eyes see our neighbors.

I grew eggplants, onions, carrots, and cauliflower. When the eggplants appeared in August they were pale purple, a strange and eerie shade. When my wife would bring our little son, he was forever wanting to pick them. There was nothing else in the garden with that color. Very many people came over to ask about them and talk to me. I recognized a few from the neighborhood. Not one had spoken to me before— and now how friendly they turned out to be. The eggplants gave them an excuse for breaking the rules and starting a conversation. How happy they seemed to have found this excuse, to let their natural friendliness out.

Those conversations tied us together. In the middle of summer someone dumped a load of tires on the garden at night, as if it were still filled with trash. A man's four rows of young corn were crushed. In an hour, we had all the tires by the curb. We were used to helping each other by then. A few weeks later, early in the evening a woman screamed, down the block from the garden. A man with a knife had taken her purse. Three men from the garden ran after him. I was surprised that I was one of them. Even more surprising, we caught him. Royce held the man to a wall with his pitchfork until the police arrived. I asked the others. Not one of us had ever chased a criminal before. And most likely we wouldn't have except near the garden. There, you felt part of a community.

I came to the United States in 1980. Cleveland is a city of immigrants. The Poles are especially well known here. I'd always heard that the Polish men were tough steelworkers and that the women cooked lots of cabbage. But I'd never known one—until the garden. She was an old woman whose space bordered mine. She had a seven-block walk to the garden, the same route I took. We spoke quite often. We both planted carrots. When her hundreds of seedlings came up in a row, I was very surprised that she did not thin them—pulling out all but one healthy-looking plant each few inches, to give them room to grow. I asked her. She looked down at them and said she knew she ought to do it, but that this task reminded her too closely of her concentration camp, where the prisoners were inspected each morning and divided into two lines—the healthy to live and the others to die. Her father, an orchestra violinist, had spoken out against the Germans, which had caused her family's arrest. When I heard her words, I realized how useless was all that I'd heard about Poles, how much richness it hid, like the worthless shell around an almond. I still do not know, or care, whether she cooks cabbage.

The garden found this out with Royce. He was young and black. He looked rather dangerous. People watched him and seemed to be relieved when he left the garden. Then he began spending more time there. We found out that he had a stutter. Then that he had two sisters, that he liked the cats that roamed through the garden, and that he worked very well with his hands. Soon all the mothers were trying to feed him. How very strange it was to watch people who would have crossed the street if they'd seen him coming a few weeks before, now giving him vegetables, more than he could eat. In return, he watered for people who were sick and fixed fences and made other repairs. He might weed your garden or use the bricks from the building that was torn down up the block to make you a brick path between your rows. He always pretended he hadn't done it. It was always a surprise. One felt honored to be chosen. He was trusted and liked—and famous, after his exploit with the pitchfork. He was not a black teenage boy. He was Royce.

In September he and a Mexican man collected many bricks from up the street and built a big barbecue. I was in the garden on Saturday when the Mexican family drove up in a truck with a dead pig in the back. They built a fire, put a heavy metal spit through the pig, and began to roast it. A bit later their friends began arriving. One brought a guitar, another played violin. They filled a folding table with food. Perhaps it was one of their birthdays, or perhaps no reason was needed for the party. It was beautiful weather, sunny but not hot. Fall was just beginning and the garden was changing from green to brown. Those of us who had come to work felt the party's spirit enter us. The smell of the roasting pig drifted out and called to everyone, gardeners or not. Soon the entire garden was filled.

It was a harvest festival, like those in India, though no one had planned it to be. People brought food and drinks and drums. I went home to get my wife and son. Watermelons from the garden were sliced open. The gardeners proudly showed off what they'd grown. We traded harvests, as we often did. And we gave food away, as we often did also—even I, a businessman, trained to give away nothing, to always make a profit. The garden provided many excuses for breaking that particular rule.

Many people spoke to me that day.

Several asked where I was from. I wondered if they knew as little about Indians as I had known about Poles. One old woman, Italian I believe, said she'd admired my eggplants for weeks and told me how happy she was to meet me. She praised them and told me how to cook them and asked all about my family. But something bothered me. Then I remembered. A year before she'd claimed that she'd received the wrong change in my store. I was called out to the register. She'd gotten quite angry and called me—despite her own accent—a dirty foreigner. Now that we were so friendly with each other I dared to remind her of this. Her eyes became huge. She apologized to me over and over again. She kept saying, "Back then, I didn't know it was *you*. . . ."

FLORENCE

My great-grandparents walked all the way from Louisiana to Colorado. That was in 1859. They were both freed slaves and they wanted to get good and far from cotton-growing country. They went over the mountains, just to be safe, and homesteaded along the Gunnison River. Which is how my grandfather and my father and my sisters and I all came to be born there, the first black family in the whole county. My father called them our seedfolks, because they were the first of our family there.

I think of them when I see any of the people who started the garden on Gibb Street. They're seedfolks too. I'm talking about that first year, before there were spigots and hoses, and the toolshed, and new soil. And before the landlords started charging more for apartments that look on the garden.

I would have been in on the garden for sure if it weren't for this arthritis in my hands. Growing up out in the country, I still miss country things. My husband's from here. He doesn't know about the smell of a hayfield and eating beans off the vine instead of from the store. I had to settle for being a watcher. I wasn't the only one. I'd see others on the fire escapes, or standing on the sidewalk like me. One day I looked up and saw a head in a window moving forward and back. It was a man who'd pulled up his rocking chair. He was watching the gardeners like TV.

My grandmother's sampler, from when she was a girl, said "Be Not Solitary, Be Not Idle." That was easy all those years in the library. Being retired, it's harder. So I try to take a walk every day, which is how I found the garden to begin with. I'd always stop there, to see what was new. I was just a watcher, but I was proud of the garden, as if it were mine. Proud and protective. I remember how mad I got when I saw a man reach through someone's fence by the sidewalk and try to grab a tomato. I said "How dare you!" He pulled back his hand and said he'd heard it was a *community* garden.

It's sad every fall, seeing it turn brown. Fewer and fewer people there. That very first year was the hardest. It had been such a wonderful change to see people making something for themselves instead of waiting for a welfare check. To see a part of the neighborhood looking *better* every day, and to smell those good smells of growing plants. The green drained away. Then the frost hit. You'd pass and hear those dry cornstalks shaking in the wind as if they were shivering. The pumpkins were about the only color left, and then the boy sold them all. Some people cut up their old plants with clippers and dug them back into the soil. A few covered their ground with leaves. But once that job was done, it was done. By November the cats were the only ones there.

That winter was a cold one. Cold as Colorado. You'd walk by the garden, covered with snow, just the fence tops sticking out, and you'd try to remember it back in July. Someone stuck a Christmas tree there in December. It stayed up until March. It's hard to tell one month from another that time of year. It's all just winter. Because of the weather I missed lots of walks. When I did get out, I couldn't go past the garden without slowing down to look, even though there was nothing growing. Sometimes there'd be one of the gardeners there, just looking too.

You can't see Canada across Lake Erie, but you know it's there. It's the same with spring. You have to have faith, especially in Cleveland. Snow in April always breaks your heart. I think we had two April snows that year. Waiting for the snow to melt was like waiting for a glacier to move. Finally, it was gone for good. The ground was back, and last year's leaves, like a bookmark showing where you'd left off. It was a joy to get out again. Just to walk without wearing a heavy coat and boots felt like flying. But the garden was still empty. I was disappointed. I suppose it was still too early to plant. I began to wonder if anyone would come. Maybe no one was interested. Or maybe the city had shut it down, or sold the lot. I was worried. Then one day I passed it—and someone was digging.

It was a little Oriental girl, with a trowel and a plastic bag of lima beans. I didn't recognize her. It didn't matter. I felt as happy inside as if I'd just seen the first swallow of spring. Then I looked up. There was the man in the rocker.

We waved and waved to each other.

FROM SEED TO *SEEDFOLKS*

by Paul Fleischman
2002

I'm a word person. When I'm eating alone,
I need to be reading something—anything.
Mere chewing seems idleness. So it was
that I found myself, five years ago, between
books, with no ghost of an idea for the next,
having lunch in a bagel shop that, astound-
ingly, offered no jam-stained, pre-owned
copy of the San Francisco *Chronicle* for
those with my affliction. Like the bagel,
serendipity is one of my four food groups.
It's usually closest at hand when farthest
from my mind. In mild disgust, I resigned
myself to a copy of a New Age tabloid—no
sports section, no movie reviews—when
something caught my eye: an article about

a local psychotherapist who used gardening to help her clients. The story mentioned that physicians in ancient Egypt prescribed garden walks for mentally ill patients. Both my heart and brain began to race. The seed for *Seedfolks* had been planted.

Books don't usually come from a single source. Like rivers, many tributaries flow into them, streams that might have begun running in childhood along with others no more than a few months old. Each book is its own braiding of waters. Sometimes authors themselves are unaware of what lies behind a book. A veil drops over our eyes when we're writing, shielding us from that realization. It might be lifted when the book is finished, or five years later, or never.

Throughout my writing life, I've worked on books designed to bring readers together. Trying to reproduce the joy and camaraderie of the early music groups and string quartets I'd played in, I'd written books of poems scored for two and four voices. I'd written books designed for readers' theater groups. Many have grown out of a germ like the article I happened on that day.

I brought home the newspaper, put the article in my file, and wrote a few notes in my idea notebook. But *Seedfolks* actually had its start many years before. My parents were both dedicated gardeners. In the summertime, in Santa Monica, California, I could pick plums, grapes, oranges, berries, loquats, apricots, figs, tangerines—and never leave my yard. Little by little, my parents had plowed under the front lawn in search of more planting space. We were—and still are—the only house in the neighborhood with a cornfield in the front yard.

My father, Sid Fleischman, is a writer of children's books as well. For him, gardening offered a recess break from his study, along with the pride and pleasure of growing one's own food. Often over dinner he would tally up the number of ingredients that had come from our soil. Writers, like gardeners, tend to be self-taught and value self-sufficiency.

I learned to write from my father, but I'm no less a product of my mother, who took her gardening skills into the community. When I was in high school, my mother volunteered at a therapeutic garden in a veterans' hospital, showing men who'd served in World War II, Korea, and Vietnam how to raise vegetables and flowers, helping to heal damaged psyches in the process.

The example of my mother's volunteerism was powerful. Over the years, she arranged book giveaways in cash-poor school districts, used her Spanish-speaking skills to tutor students in English, and, in her last years, learned Braille so as to translate books for the blind. The conflict between my parents' spheres—the printed page and the wider world—is an ancient one for me. I've solved it by keeping a foot in both. Following my mother's lead, I've tutored foreign-language speakers, taught violin and string figures, delivered library books to shut-ins. In an earlier book of mine, a character who's lost her mother vows to keep her alive by becoming her. I've found myself doing the same. My own mother died a few years before *Seedfolks*. She was a large part of the lure of the idea. A book about the healing power of plants would keep her flame lit.

I'd heard about community gardens—plots of land, usually in large cities, where anyone can grow food and flowers. Such a setting would offer a more varied cast than a therapeutic garden: women, children, teenagers, people from every corner of the world. I began researching. A marvelous magnetism takes place when an idea for a book takes hold. Newspapers and magazines suddenly seemed filled with references to community gardens. A friend of mine took a job at a local garden for the homeless. Another friend who'd helped found a community garden in Boston made me a tape of reminiscences. I read books. I toured gardens, taking notes.

I knew immigration would be central to the book. "Seedfolks" is an old term for ancestors. I'd come across the word many years before and written it in my notebook as a possible title. My thought at the time was to collect actual accounts of first-generation immigrants to the United States, those who were the founders of their families here. The book had never come to pass, but the title remained on my list and on my mind. Suddenly, I had a book to go with it. For a writer, the few words of a title can be harder than writing the rest of the book. To have an idea that comes ready-made with a title is like buying a house that's already furnished.

Though my own family had immigrated generations before—one of my mother's relations had been tried as a witch in Massachusetts—I wanted to focus on recent immigrants. This led me to choose Cleveland as a setting, a city famous for its foreign-born population in the past and now absorbing immigrants from new quarters of the globe. Famous as well for its harsh, white winters, Cleveland would be a place with a short summer, where the sight of green would be especially precious. Not to be forgotten in the decision were a number of friends of mine who lived or had lived there. Can you see Canada across Lake Erie? That's the sort of question I'd likely spend weeks fruitlessly trying to track down in books—and the sort that a friend on the phone could answer at once.

Ideas are everywhere. As my father says, the trick is turning them into something. What would be the book's shape and story? I decided to concentrate on the garden's first year—like the infancy of a baby or a plant, a time of dramatic growth. I also knew I wanted to tell its history through a variety of characters, each with a distinctive voice. I'd done this in *Bull Run*, my previous book, an account of the Civil War's first battle told through 16 points of view. The monologues in that book had been very short, each character speaking several times. I have an aversion to repeating myself and wanted something different this time—longer speeches, closer to short stories, with characters only speaking once, yet appearing in the background of other speakers' accounts, presaging their entrances and following up their exits.

Those characters began taking shape. Some, like sailors awaiting a ship, had haunted my notebook for years but had never found their way into a book. Others popped up out of nowhere. Research is a wonderful push-pull proposition. You go looking for facts and return with fiction. I read that a few gardens had problems with people raising produce for profit, and came up with Virgil's father, the would-be lettuce baron. I came across a mention of a support group for teen mothers taking part in a garden, and invented Maricela. Sae Young came from a newspaper article I'd seen years before about a teacher who'd been assaulted, lost all trust in people, and hadn't left his apartment for years.

Other characters were aspects of me. Sam, who greets everyone he sees, came from the year I spent in an ingrown Omaha neigborhood. Mine was the only beard on the block. Rocks were thrown at me on my first bicycle ride. Like Sam, I began going out of my way to make small talk with grocery store clerks and people at the bus stop, showing them they had no reason to fear me—or, by extension, others who looked different.

"Write what you know" is common advice for writers. In fact, I'm not much of a gardener myself. I read up on soil and pests and propagation, but it soon became clear to me that the focus of the book was people, not plants. To experience some of what my characters were going through, however, I planted a long row of bush beans in my yard midway through the writing. Suddenly, I understood. I felt pulled out of bed to check on them every morning and gave them a last look every night. Every milestone felt worthy of celebration: the first cracks in the earth, the first sprouts poking through like bird beaks, the first flower, the first bean. I picked off bugs with fierce maternal vigilance and laid an aria of invective on pillaging rabbits. Truly, as Nora says, a garden is a soap opera growing out of the ground.

The Vietnam vet, who dropped thousands of tiny seeds on his soil to make up for the thousands of bombs he'd dropped, never made it out of my notebook. Nor did the alcoholic gardener who spoke to his plants. A book, like a plant, finds its own shape. I feared young adult readers wouldn't sit still for a book about a garden and for a time I lost faith and put the book aside. When I returned to it, I felt that it had to be shorter, so as not to bore my readers and to avoid repeating certain character types. And unlike *Bull Run*, the book would be open-ended, with the outcome of various characters' dramas left to readers' imaginations.

The book came out, with its lovely jacket and illustrations. Books are quite like seeds; the writer never knows exactly what will come up. Some are yanked out by hostile reviewers, others please passersby and spread extravagantly. Like teenagers, successful books move out of the house and take on a life all their own, received in distant homes, traveling far, being translated into other tongues. Writers know nothing of these journeys except through fan mail—the postcards sent home by the book. I've followed *Seedfolks*'s progress through these.

Like the ancient Egyptians, we recognize that contact with nature can heal. Hours after the 9/11 attacks in New York, scores of people were standing in wait for the gates of the Brooklyn Botanic Garden to open. The city's public gardens waived admission fees and were thronged with those seeking solace and serenity. In the uprush of altruism, we also saw that a sense of community—that we are known, that we care, that we will be cared for—

provides an even greater solace.

I sense that we all have hidden stores of generosity that find no outlet except in such moments of disaster. This was the marvel of the community gardens I visited. They were oases in the urban landscape of fear, places where people could safely offer trust, helpfulness, charity, without need of an earthquake or hurricane. Television, I'm afraid, has isolated us more than race, class, or ethnicity. Community gardens are places where people rediscover not only generosity, but the pleasure of coming together. I salute all those who give their time and talents to rebuilding that sense of belonging. It's a potent seed. "I have great faith in a seed," wrote Thoreau. "Convince me that you have a seed there, and I am prepared to expect wonders."

Also by Paul Fleischman...

Bull Run
Pb 0-06-440588-5

Through 60 monologues, 16 characters describe their experiences in the Civil War's first major battle.

The Borning Room
Pb 0-06-447099-7

A 19th-century Ohio girl's autobiography told through scenes centered in her home's borning room.

Saturnalia
Pb 0-06-447089-X

Set during the Puritans' Indian Wars, two casts of characters inhabit Boston's streets—one by day, the other by night—linked by a captured Narraganset boy.

Time Train
Pb 0-06-443351-X

On a trip to study dinosaurs, a class finds its train transporting them not simply to Utah—but to the Jurassic.

Joyful Noise
Illustrated by Eric Beddows · Hc 0-06-021852-5 · Pb 0-06-446093-2

The Newbery Medal–winning classic collection of poems for two voices detailing the inner lives of insects, from book lice to whirligig beetles.

I Am Phoenix
Illustrated by Ken Nutt · Pb 0-06-446092-4

Companion to Joyful Noise, a collection of poems for two voices celebrating the world of birds.

The Half-a-Moon Inn
Pb 0-06-440364-5

A mute boy sets off in search of his mother, only to find himself a captive of the Half-a-Moon Inn and its dream-reading mistress.

www.harperchildrens.com · www.paulfleischman.net

HarperTrophy®
An Imprint of HarperCollinsPublishers